To Jonathan

SIMON & SCHUSTER BOOKS FOR YOUNG READERS
An imprint of Simon & Schuster Children's Publishing Division
1230 Avenue of the Americas, New York, New York 10020
Copyright © 2019 by Jessica Lanan • All rights reserved, including the right of reproduction in whole or in part in any form. • SIMON & SCHUSTER BOOKS FOR YOUNG READERS is a trademark of Simon & Schuster, Inc. • For information about special discounts for bulk purchases, please contact Simon & Schuster Special Sales at 1-866-506-1949 or business@simonandschuster.com. The Simon & Schuster Speakers Bureau can bring authors to your live event. • For more information or to book an event, contact the Simon & Schuster Speakers Bureau at 1-866-248-3049 or visit our website at www.simonspeakers.com. • Book design by Krista Vossen • The text for this book was set in Kepler. The illustrations for this book were rendered in watercolor and gouache on Saunders Waterford paper. • Manufactured in China • 0219 SCP • First Edition • 10 9 8 7 6 5 4 3 2 1
Library of Congress Cataloging-in-Publication Data • Names: Lanan, Jessica, author, illustrator. • Title: The fisherman and the whale / Jessica Lanan. • Description: First edition. | New York : Simon & Schuster Books for Young Readers, [2019] | Summary: A wordless picture book in which a fisherman finds a whale caught in fishing nets and sets it free. Includes author's note about the environmental impact of contemporary commercial fishing practices. • Identifiers: LCCN 2018035262| ISBN 9781534415744 (hardcover) | ISBN 9781534415751 (ebook) • Subjects: | CYAC: Whales—Fiction. | Fishers—Fiction. | Wildlife rescue—Fiction. | Stories without words. • Classification: LCC PZ7.1.L268 Fis 2019 | DDC • |E]—dc23
LC record available at https://lccn.loc.gov/2018035262

The Fisherman & the Whale

Jessica Lanan

Simon & Schuster Books for Young Readers
New York London Toronto Sydney New Delhi

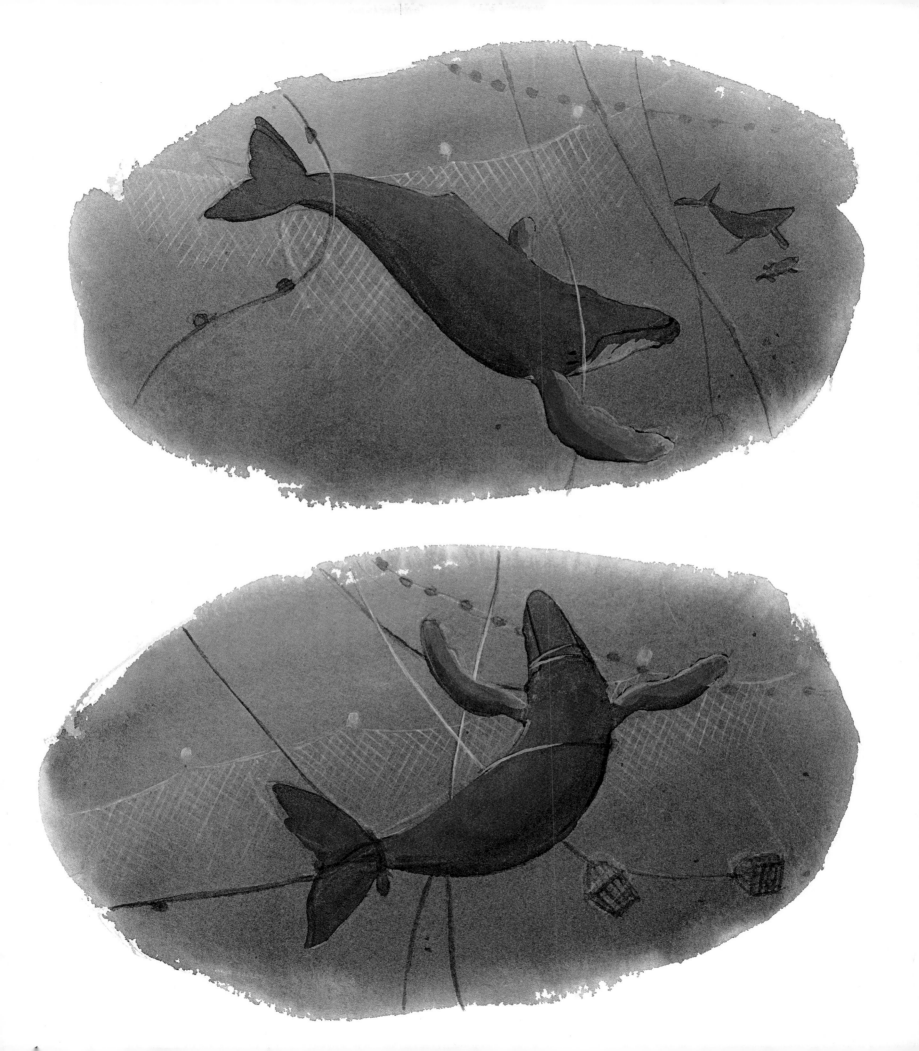

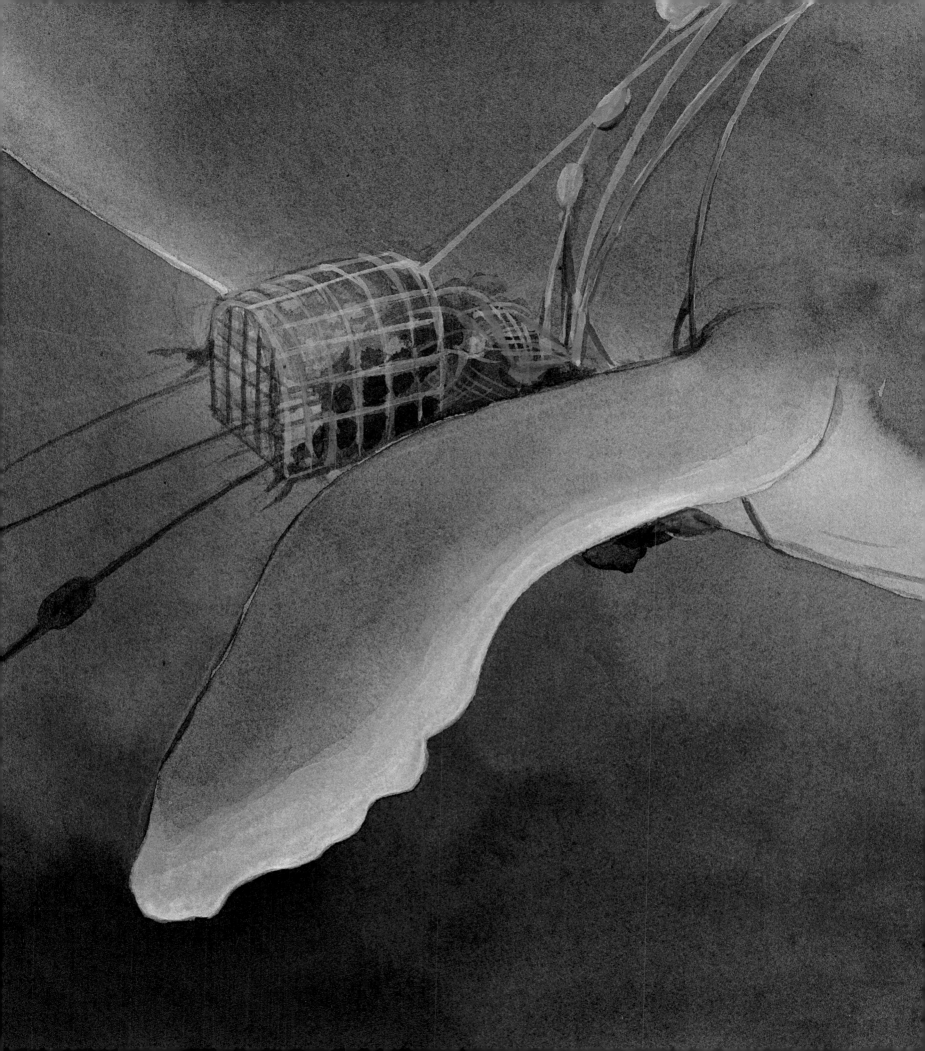

AUTHOR'S NOTE

According to World Wildlife Fund, over 300,000 whales, dolphins, and porpoises die each year after becoming entangled in commercial fishing nets. The devastation of whales and other life on our planet is a problem effected by all of us, not just when we buy and eat fish, but whenever we thoughtlessly consume and discard. This cycle has unfortunately become one of our favorite human pastimes. I hope that I can help shed light on how our collective habits can add up to profound environmental damage, but this damage can still be overcome by our innate individual capacity for care and empathy. It is very important to me that this story is not just the tale of one whale's rescue, but a reflection of the environmental harm that we humans unwittingly cause and the deep empathy that can reconnect us to other living things across the bounds of size, habitat, and species.

The boat and method of fishing that I have depicted here is loosely based on the technique known as "purse seining," often used for catching salmon. I have illustrated a simplified version of this technique for reasons of composition and clarity. In reality, the purse seining method requires the efforts of a crew of four, plus a skiff. The net is stretched between the two boats, then the boats converge in order to wrap the net around the school of fish. The whale in this story becomes ensnared in creel lines, a type of fishing line used for catching lobsters, prawns, or crabs.

I would like to note that it is very dangerous and possibly illegal to approach a whale or attempt to get into the water to help it. Please suspend your disbelief and read this story as a fable rather than a literal guide on whale rescue. This story is not intended to condone or encourage rescue attempts by anyone other than the proper professional wildlife rescue authorities. If you ever see a whale that you suspect may be entangled, call the authorities as soon as possible. They will be able to rescue the whale more quickly than you could, and with less risk of harm to whale or human. For more information about whale entanglement, please visit iwc.int/entanglement.